Who Lives on the Farm?

Illustrated by Lisa Bonforte

A GOLDEN BOOK • NEW YORK

Western Publishing Company, Inc.
Racine, Wisconsin 53404

Who lives on the farm?
Chickens and baby chicks live here,
and a rooster who stands on a fence and crows.
The hens lay their eggs in the chicken house.

Ducks and geese also live on the farm. Ducks and geese like water, so they spend most of their time at the pond.

Who else lives on the farm?
There are cows on the farm,
and a bull who stays in his own pasture.

On this farm there are many riding horses, too, and a strong, brown mule who helps with the farm work.

The horses sleep in the stable.
And the mare stays there with
her newborn foal.

Who else lives on the farm?
White, woolly sheep live here.
A big, brown sheepdog makes sure
that none of the baby lambs get lost.

Goats live on the farm, too.
Baby goats are called kids.
The kids drink their mother's milk
until they are big enough to eat grass.

Who lives in the pigsty?
Plump, pink pigs live there.
Pigs like to eat. On hot days they
also like to roll in the cool mud.

A flock of turkeys strut around the barnyard, showing off their feathers.

A family of cats live in the hayloft.
They chase away the mice that eat
the farmer's grain.

Wild animals live in the fields
and woods. They come out to look for
food when the farm animals are sleeping.
Who lives on the farm?
All kinds of animals live on the farm.